There was once a farmer who had a donkey that had worked for him for many years. The donkey grew old and could not work any more, so the farmer thought about selling him.

'It's time for me to leave,' said the donkey. 'I still have a fine voice. I will go to the famous city of Bremen and sing with the town band.'

And he set off along the highway.

He had not gone far when he met a dog, lying in the road, and panting as if he was very tired.

'What is the matter?' said the donkey.

'Ah,' said the dog, 'I have grown old and weak, and my master thinks about getting rid of me. Now I have run away. But where shall I go? And what shall I do?'

'Come with me,' said the donkey. 'I am on my way to Bremen. You can bark and I can bray, and together we can sing in the town band.'

And so they went along the highway happily together.

After they had travelled a little way, they met a cat, who was looking very sad.

'What is wrong?' said the donkey.

'Ah,' said the cat, 'I can't catch mice any more and my mistress says that I am useless. So I decided to run away. But what will happen to me now?'

'Come with us to Bremen,' said the donkey. 'You can miaow, the dog can bark, I can bray, and together we can sing in the town band.'

And so all three went cheerfully along the highway.

Not long afterwards they came upon a cockerel, perched upon a gate, and crowing with all his might.

'Why do you crow so loudly?' said the donkey.

'The farmer's wife says I am too old to be useful any more,' said the cockerel. 'So I am making as much noise as I can before she puts me in the cooking-pot.'

'Why don't you come to Bremen with us?' said the donkey. 'You can crow, the cat can miaow, the dog can bark, I can bray, and together we can sing in the town band.'

And so all four went along the highway, singing together.

However, time was getting on and the four friends knew they couldn't get to Bremen that day. When night fell, they came to a forest and decided to sleep there.

The donkey and the dog lay down under a tall tree, while the cat climbed up into the branches.

The cockerel flew up to the top of the tree and looked around.
In the distance he saw a spark of light.

'Friends,' he said, 'I think there's a house nearby.
Let's go and see if we can find some food.'

The animals all agreed, so off they went together. Soon they came upon a house with a bright light streaming from the windows.

The donkey went up to the house and peeped in through
a window.

'What do you see in there?' said the cockerel.

'What do I see?' said the donkey. 'I see a table full of good
things to eat and five fierce robbers standing around it.'

'I'd love some of that food,' said the dog.
'So would I,' said the cockerel. 'But how can we get in?'

At last the cat thought of a plan. The donkey put his front legs on the window-sill, the dog got on his back, the cat climbed on to the dog, and the cockerel flew up and perched on the cat.

'Now!' said the cockerel. 'Let us all sing together!'

The donkey brayed, the dog barked, the cat miaowed, and the cockerel screamed. Then they all broke through the window at once and came tumbling into the room with a terrible clatter.

The robbers were so frightened that
they ran out of the house as fast as
their legs would carry them.

The four friends burst out laughing and tucked in to the
food on the table. When they had eaten everything in
sight, they settled down and went to sleep.

Meanwhile, one of the robbers crept
back inside the house. It was so
dark that he trod on the cat who
spat at him, he tripped over the dog
who bit him, he bumped into the
donkey who kicked him, and then
the cockerel flew on top of him,
crowing away.

The robber was terrified
and ran back to the
others. 'A terrible old
witch spat at me, a fierce
man stabbed me, a huge
monster kicked me, and a
demon screamed in my
ear.' At this the robbers all
ran away and were never
seen again.

The friends were all so pleased with the house that they
stayed there and lived happily together. And they never
did go and sing in the Bremen town band.

Oxford University Press, Great Clarendon Street, Oxford OX2 6DP
Oxford is a trade mark of Oxford University Press
Copyright © Brian Wildsmith 1999
First published 1999
Reprinted in hardback 2000 (twice)
Adapted from a story by the Brothers Grimm
All rights reserved. ISBN 0 19 279034 X (hardback)
ISBN 0 19 272394 4 (paperback)
Typeset by Mike Brain
Printed in China